by Crystal Bowman
illustrated by Karen Maizel

ZondervanPublishingHouse
Grand Rapids, Michigan

A Division of HarperCollins*Publishers*

Jonathan James Says, "I Can Be Brave"

Requests for information should be addressed to:
Zondervan Publishing House
Grand Rapids, Michigan 49530

Library of Congress Cataloging-in-Publication Data

Bowman, Crystal.
Jonathan James says, "I can be brave" / by Crystal Bowman.
p. cm. — (Jonathan James)
Summary: Jonathan, a young rabbit, faces his first day at school, his first night in a new bedroom, and other new and frightening experiences, but he is comforted by the love of his family and the presence of God.
ISBN: 0-310-49591-1
[1. Rabbits—Fiction. 2. Fear—Fiction. 3. Christian life—Fiction.] I. Title. II. Series: Bowman, Crystal. Jonathan James.
PZ7.B6834Jo 1995
[E]—dc20 95-2127
CIP
AC

Edited by Lori J. Walburg and Leslie Kimmelman
Cover design by Steven M. Scott
Art direction by Chris Gannon
Illustrations and interior design by Karen Maizel

95 96 97 98 99 /❖ DP / 10 9 8 7 6 5 4 3 2 1

To my parents,
Harold and Gerene Langejans,
with love and appreciation
for all they have taught me
—C. B.

For Stan,
my steel girder
—K. M.

CONTENTS

THE NEW BEDROOM

It was bedtime for Jonathan James.
He was so excited!
Tonight he would sleep
in his new bedroom.
Jonathan had shared a bedroom
with his little sister, Kelly.
But now he was big enough
for his very own room.
"Having my own room will be fun,"
said Jonathan.
Jonathan took a bath
and brushed his teeth.
Then he got into bed.

He climbed under the blankets.
Father read him a story.
Mother prayed with him
and gave him a kiss.
"Good night, J.J.," said Mother.
"We love you," said Father.
"Good night," said Jonathan.
Mother and Father
turned out the light.

Jonathan closed his eyes.
Then he opened his eyes.
He could not fall asleep.
He missed Kelly.
He did not like being alone.
He did not like the dark.
Jonathan was afraid.
"I will turn on the light,"
said Jonathan.
"Then I will not be afraid."

Jonathan turned on the light.
"That is better!" he said.
Jonathan looked around
his new room.
He looked at the animals
on his dresser.
The animals made shadows
on the wall.
Jonathan did not like the shadows.

The light was too bright.

It hurt his eyes.

Jonathan turned out the light.

Now his room was dark again.

Jonathan was afraid.

"I will take my animals

to bed with me," said Jonathan.

"Then I will not be afraid."

Jonathan put his animals in bed.

He closed his eyes.

But he could not sleep.

His bed was too crowded.
His fuzzy monkey
made his nose itch.
Jonathan put the animals
back on his dresser.
"I know," said Jonathan.
"I will crawl under my bed.
Then I will not be afraid."
Jonathan crawled under his bed.
But he could not fall asleep.
The floor was hard.

Jonathan was cold.
He got back into bed.
Finally, he was so tired
that he fell asleep.
The next morning,
Jonathan woke up.
He went into the kitchen
for breakfast.
“Good morning, J.J.,” said Mother.
“Here’s a waffle for you.”
“You look tired,” said Father.
“I did not sleep well,”
Jonathan told them.
“Oh?” said Mother.
“Why not?” asked Father.
“It was dark,” said Jonathan.
“I was afraid.”

"Yes," Father agreed.
"It is dark at night."
"Very dark!"
said Mother.
"But I am not afraid."
"No," said Father.
"I am not afraid, either.
I know that God watches
over us at night."
"Yes, He does," Mother said.
"He does not go to sleep."
"Are you sure?" asked Jonathan.
"Yes," Mother answered.
"Very sure," Father answered.
"That is nice to know,"
said Jonathan.

That night, Jonathan took a bath
and brushed his teeth.
Father read him a story.
Mother prayed with him
and gave him a kiss.
"Good night, J.J.," said Mother.
"We love you," said Father.
"Good night," said Jonathan.
Jonathan closed his eyes.
He did not turn on his light.
He did not get his animals.
He did not crawl under his bed.
"God is awake," Jonathan
told himself.
"He is watching over me."
Jonathan fell asleep.

J.J.

FIRST GRADE

Jonathan was taking a bath.
Summer vacation was over.
Tomorrow he would go
to first grade.
Jonathan liked summer vacation.
He did not want to go to school.

"Time to get out," said Mother.
"Okay," said Jonathan.
"But I am not going
to school tomorrow."
"What?" asked Mother.
"I am not going to school,"
Jonathan said again.
"Why?" asked Mother.
"Because I want to go to the beach,"
Jonathan replied.
"I want to go for bike rides
and eat ice cream.
I want to go to the park
to swing and slide."

"But J.J.," said Mother,
"you like school.
You like to draw pictures
and sing songs.
You like to write numbers
and letters.
And you like playing
with your friends at recess."
"I know," said Jonathan.
"But first grade will be different.
I will be at school all day.
I will get tired."
"You will be fine," said Mother.
"I will miss you," said Jonathan.
"I will be all alone."

“You will not be alone,”
said Mother.
“You will be with your teacher.
You will be with your friends.
And God will be with you too.
You will like first grade.
You will see.”

The next morning,
Jonathan got ready for school.
He put on his blue shirt
and his new tennis shoes.
He carried his new lunch box.
It was bright green with
yellow and red letters all over it.

At school, Jonathan met
his new teacher, Mrs. Morris.
She was nice.
Then it was time for Mother
to go home.
Jonathan did not want her to leave,
but he was brave.
Jonathan knew he was not alone.
He was with Mrs. Morris,
and he was with his friends.
And God was with him, too.

Mrs. Morris gave him
some paper and crayons.
Jonathan drew a picture.
At the top he wrote his name,
all by himself.
After lunch, Jonathan sang songs
and listened to a story.
But the best part of the day
was playing with his friends
at recess.

After school, Jonathan gave Mother
the picture he drew.
“What a beautiful picture, J. J.,”
said Mother.
“Did you have fun today?”
“Oh, yes!” said Jonathan.
“I drew pictures and sang songs.
I listened to a story,
and I played with my friends
at recess.
May I go again tomorrow?”
“Of course!” Mother laughed.

Mother was right.

Jonathan liked first grade.

LOST

Wednesday was shopping day.
After school, Mother took Jonathan
and Kelly to the grocery store.
Jonathan liked helping Mother
get the groceries.
Today Mother let him
pick out some ice cream.
He chose chocolate swirl.

Then they stopped
at the meat counter.
“Well, hello, Jonathan,”
said Mr. Bob.
“Hi, Mr. Bob,” said Jonathan.
“What will you have today?”
asked Mr. Bob.

Jonathan pretended to think.
"Ten hamburgers!" he said.
Mr. Bob and Mother laughed.
"Please give me two pounds
of hamburger meat," said Mother.
Mr. Bob wrapped the meat
and gave it to Jonathan.
He winked.
"There are your ten hamburgers,"
he said.
"Thank you," said Jonathan.
He put the meat in the cart.

Then Jonathan went down
another aisle
with Mother and Kelly.
He saw some toy cars
hanging on hooks from the wall.
"May I look at the cars?"
asked Jonathan.
"Yes," said Mother,
"but just for a little while."

Jonathan looked at a blue car
and a red car.
He looked at a green truck.
Then he saw a yellow fire truck.
Jonathan liked the yellow fire truck.
"We must get our food now,"
said Mother.
"I want to look at the fire truck,"
said Jonathan.
"You've looked long enough,"
Mother told him.
"Okay," said Jonathan,
"I'm coming."
Jonathan put the yellow fire truck
back on the hook.

But when he looked up

Mother was gone.

He did not see her anywhere.

Jonathan was all alone.

He started to cry.

Then he remembered
his friend, Mr. Bob.
Jonathan went back
to the meat counter.

"I can't find my mother!"
Jonathan sobbed.
"Don't worry," said Mr. Bob.
He patted Jonathan on his back.
"I will help you find her."

Mr. Bob talked into a telephone.
His voice boomed through the store.
"Would Jonathan's mother
please come to the meat counter?"
called Mr. Bob.
Jonathan waited with Mr. Bob.
Soon he saw Mother and Kelly
coming toward him.
He was so happy!
He ran up to Mother
and hugged her.
"I thought you were behind me,"
said Mother.
"I looked all over for you.
I was so worried!"
Mother thanked Mr. Bob.
Then she finished her shopping.

That night, Jonathan told Father
what had happened.
“Being lost was scary!”
said Jonathan.
“I’m sure it was!” said Father.
“But you can never
be lost from God.
God used Mr. Bob to help you.”

“That is good,” said Jonathan.

“Yes,” said Father, “that is good.”

“Can we have some
chocolate swirl ice cream?”
asked Jonathan.

“I picked it out myself.”

“Good for you!” said Father.
“Let’s eat!”

WEEKEND AT GRANDMA'S

Mother was in her bedroom.
She was putting her clothes
into a suitcase.
"Why are you packing your clothes?"
asked Jonathan.
"Father and I are going to a cabin,"
said Mother.
"It is our wedding anniversary."
"Who is going to stay with us?"
asked Jonathan.
"You and Kelly
are going to Grandma's house,"
Mother told him.
Jonathan liked going
to Grandma's house.

He liked her big swing.
He liked her big box of toys.
And he liked her apple muffins.
But Jonathan had never
stayed overnight
at Grandma's house.
"How long will we be there?"
asked Jonathan.
"Just one night," said Mother.
"You and Kelly will have fun."
"Maybe," said Jonathan.

After school on Friday,
they went to Grandma's house.
Mother and Father
kissed them good-bye.
Jonathan felt like crying.

"I know," said Grandma,
"let's make some muffins."
"Yippee!" said Kelly.
"I guess," said Jonathan.

Jonathan poured the flour
into a bowl.
He spilled some on the counter.
Kelly dropped an egg on the floor.
Grandma didn't mind.
"We will just clean it up,"
she said.
Grandma put the muffins
into the oven.
They smelled yummy.
They tasted even better.

"When do we have a bath?"
asked Jonathan.
"No need for baths at my house,"
Grandma said.
"When do we go to bed?"
asked Jonathan.
"We will stay up all night,"
Grandma said.
"What are we going to do?"
asked Jonathan.
"Let's pretend," said Grandma.
"We can go camping.
I will get some blankets."
"Good idea!" Jonathan agreed.
"Let's go swimming in the river,"
Grandma suggested.
"Oh, yes!" said Jonathan.

Grandma filled the bathtub
with water.
Kelly went in first.
Then Jonathan went in.
"When I was a girl," said Grandma,
"I washed my hair in the river."
"May I wash my hair in the river?"
asked Jonathan.
"Of course," said Grandma.
Jonathan washed his hair
and swam in the river.

"It's time to dry off now,"
said Grandma.
"Let's pretend it's bedtime."
Jonathan and Kelly
put on their pajamas.
"How about a story?"
Grandma asked.
"Yes," said Jonathan, "a Bible story."
"I am happy that you love Jesus,"
said Grandma.
"When I was little,
my mother told me about Jesus.
I told your father about Jesus.
Now he tells you about Jesus."

"That is the way life goes,"
said Jonathan.
"Yes," said Grandma.
"That is the way life goes."
Grandma started reading
a Bible story.
Jonathan and Kelly fell fast asleep.
Grandma went to bed.

On Saturday, Father and Mother
came to Grandma's house.
"Did you have fun?" asked Father.
"Oh, yes!" Jonathan answered.
"We made muffins,
and we went camping.
We stayed up all night.

We didn't even take a bath."
Jonathan winked at Grandma.
Grandma winked at Jonathan.
"Come again soon," Grandma said.
"I will!" said Jonathan.
"Me too!" said Kelly.

Read up on the adventures of Jonathan James!

Jonathan James Says, "I Can Be Brave"

Book 1 ISBN 0-310-49591-1

Jonathan James is afraid. His new bedroom is too dark. He's going into first grade. And he has to stay at Grandma's overnight for the first time. What should he do? These four lively, humorous stories will show new readers that sometimes things that seemed scary can actually be fun.

Jonathan James Says, "Let's Be Friends"

Book 2 ISBN 0-310-49601-2

Jonathan James is making new friends! In four easy-to-read stories, Jonathan meets a missionary, a physically challenged boy, and a new neighbor. New readers will learn important lessons about friendship. And they will learn that our friends like us just for being who we are.

Jonathan James Says, "I Can Help"

Book 3 ISBN 0-310-49611-X

Jonathan James is growing up–and that means he can help! In four chapters written especially for new readers, Jonathan James learns to pitch in and help his family–sometimes successfully, sometimes not. Young readers will learn that they, too, have ways they can help.

Jonathan James Says, "Let's Play Ball"

Book 4 ISBN 0-310-49621-7

Jonathan James wants to learn how to play baseball. Who will teach him? Will he ever hit the ball? Four fun-filled chapters show young readers that, with practice, they too can succeed in whatever they try.

Look for all the books in the Jonathan James series at your local Christian bookstore.

ZondervanPublishingHouse
5300 Patterson S.E. • Grand Rapids, MI 49530

Crystal Bowman writes from her home in Grand Rapids, Michigan, where she lives with her husband and three children. “My children give me most of my ideas!” she says. Besides writing stories, she also composes funny poems and lyrics for children’s music. Crystal is often a “special guest author” in local schools, where she enjoys sharing the joy of writing with children.

Karen Maizel illustrates from her home near Cleveland, Ohio, where she lives with her husband and three daughters. “My childhood drawings were very ordinary,” she says. “But God’s gift to me was the love of drawing. Through lots of practice, I got better and better.” Karen’s goal is to bring Jesus to young minds and hearts through her pictures.

Crystal and Karen would love to hear from you. You may write them at:

Author Relations
Zondervan Publishing House
5300 Patterson Ave., S.E.
Grand Rapids, MI 49530